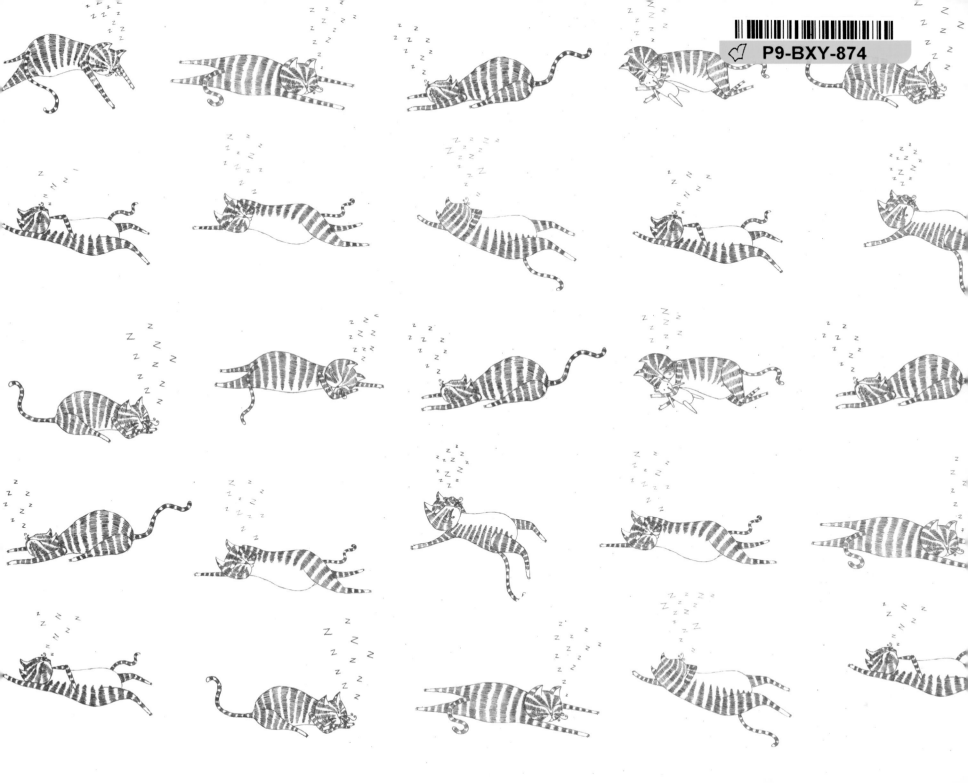

The AMAZING HAMWEENIE

Patty Bowman

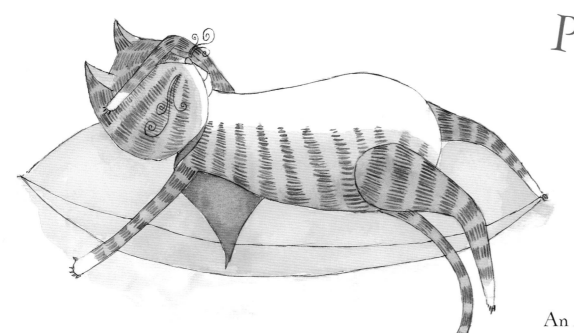

PHILOMEL BOOKS
An Imprint of Penguin Group (USA) Inc.

For my parents

. . . and my cat Bandini.

PHILOMEL BOOKS

A division of Penguin Young Readers Group.   Published by The Penguin Group.
Penguin Group (USA) Inc., 375 Hudson Street, New York, NY 10014, U.S.A.   Penguin Group (Canada), 90 Eglinton Avenue East, Suite 700, Toronto,
Ontario M4P 2Y3, Canada (a division of Pearson Penguin Canada Inc.).   Penguin Books Ltd, 80 Strand, London WC2R 0RL, England.   Penguin Ireland, 25 St.
Stephen's Green, Dublin 2, Ireland (a division of Penguin Books Ltd).   Penguin Group (Australia), 250 Camberwell Road, Camberwell, Victoria 3124, Australia
(a division of Pearson Australia Group Pty Ltd).   Penguin Books India Pvt Ltd, 11 Community Centre, Panchsheel Park, New Delhi - 110 017, India.   Penguin Group (NZ),
67 Apollo Drive, Rosedale, Auckland 0632, New Zealand (a division of Pearson New Zealand Ltd).   Penguin Books (South Africa) (Pty) Ltd, 24 Sturdee Avenue, Rosebank,
Johannesburg 2196, South Africa.   Penguin Books Ltd, Registered Offices: 80 Strand, London WC2R 0RL, England.

Edited by Michael Green and Julia Johnson.   Design by Semadar Megged.   Text set in 20-point Oneleigh.
The illustrations are rendered in pen and ink and watercolors on watercolor paper.
Library of Congress Cataloging-in-Publication Data
Bowman, Patty.   The amazing Hamweenie / Patty Bowman.   p. cm.   Summary: Hamweenie the cat dreams of fame but is continually brought back to reality
by the torment of his life in an apartment.   [1. Cats—Fiction. 2. Apartment houses—Fiction. 3. Imagination—Fiction.] I. Title.
PZ7.B6856Am 2012   [E]—dc23   2011036840
ISBN 978-0-399-25688-2
3 5 7 9 10 8 6 4 2

In the big city,

in an apartment,

there lives a cat named Hamweenie.

He dreams of grandeur

and stardom,

of being loved the world over
and idolized by children.

Nevertheless,

fate has been cruel to Hamweenie.

His living conditions

are atrocious.

Often he is poisoned

and even starved.

Don't you know who I am?

I demand you release me.

He strives to perfect his skills,

but at every turn, someone is there to sabotage him.

His efforts to stay out of sight

prove futile.

Undeterred by the agonizing abuse

that awaits him,

He bestows his wrath

with merciless abandon.

And no matter how clever

his schemes to escape are,

it seems all his attempts are made in vain.

As punishment, he is tortured in unimaginable ways.

So Hamweenie bides his time . . .

waiting for this endless array of
horrors and injustice to end.

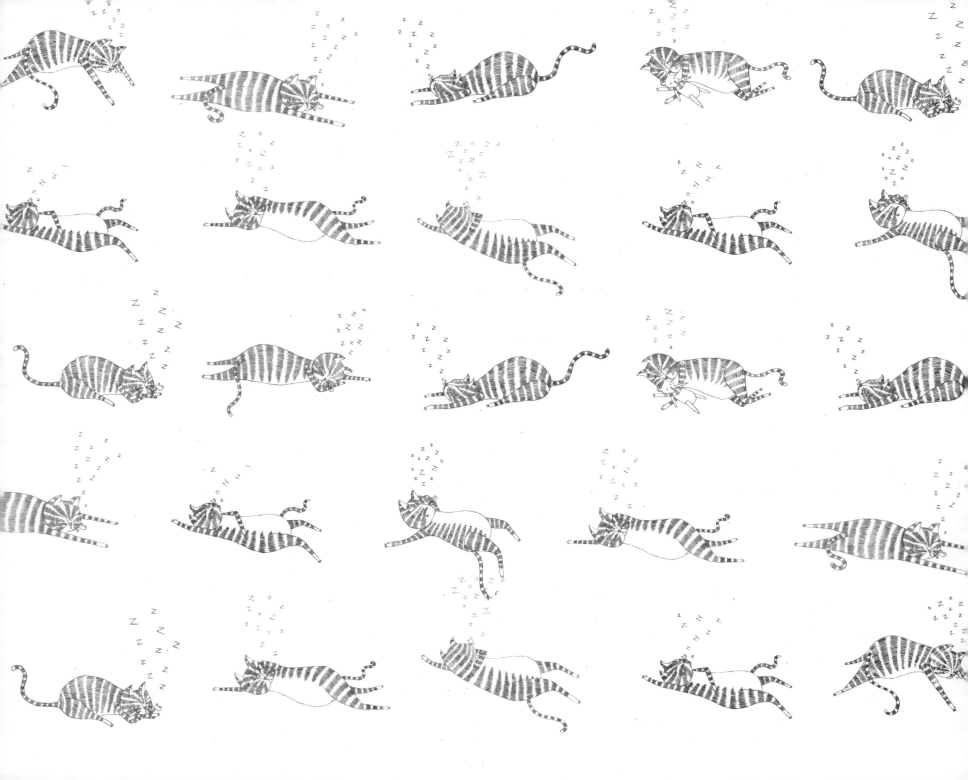